Kori Jai and the Big Girl Bed

Written By: Meiha Maxwell

Copyright © 2018 Meiha Maxwell
All rights reserved.
ISBN-10: 1719214999
ISBN-13: 978-1719214995

Dedication
This book is dedicated to my beautiful Kori Jai. You are my inspiration. Mommy loves you more than you will ever know. I can't wait to see you fly Baby Girl.

Kori Jai and the Big Girl Bed

Written By: Meiha Maxwell
Illustrations By: Jayde Coppenbarger

Kori Jai is the queen of her crib. As the day comes to a close, the adventures of the night are just beginning. Mommy tucks Kori in and cracks the door.

As mommy's footsteps finally reach the end of the hallway, Kori springs out from under her blanket and the blanket turns into a magic carpet.

Kori hops on the carpet and flies around the room. She ducks as she approaches the upside down lily flowers. Kori points her finger into the distance. The blanket catches speed and poof, through a cloud of cotton candy she goes.

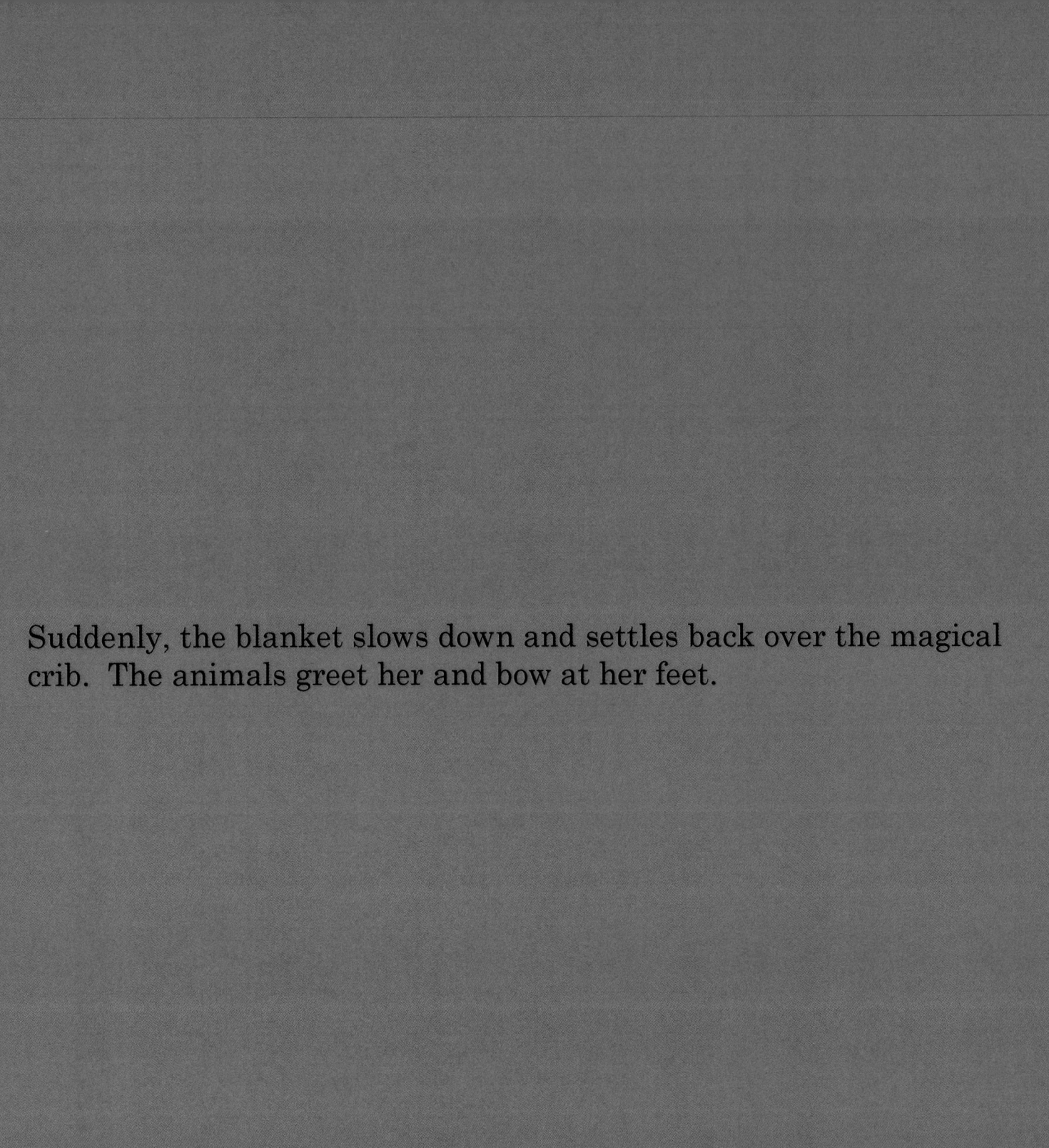

Suddenly, the blanket slows down and settles back over the magical crib. The animals greet her and bow at her feet.

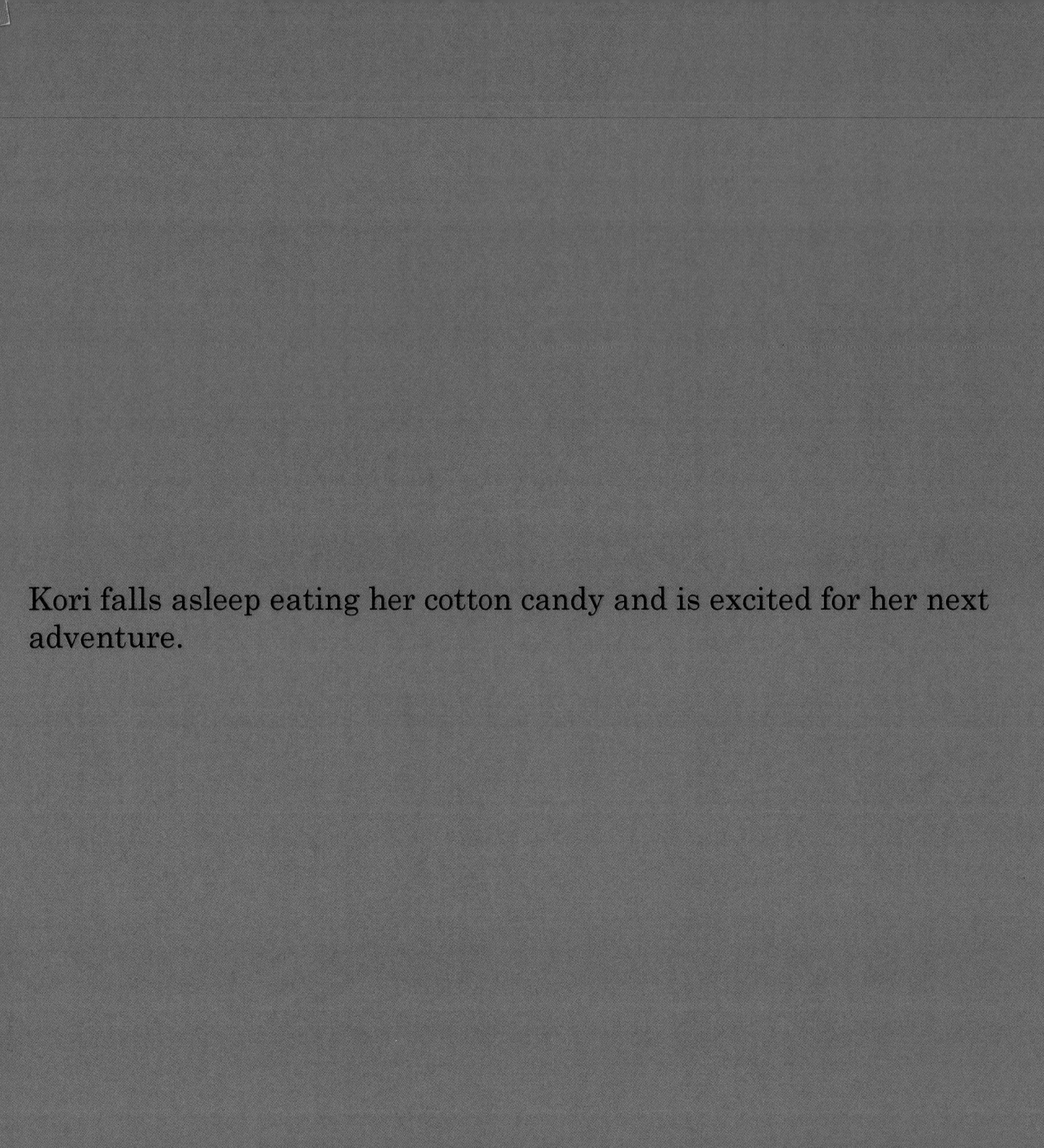

Kori falls asleep eating her cotton candy and is excited for her next adventure.

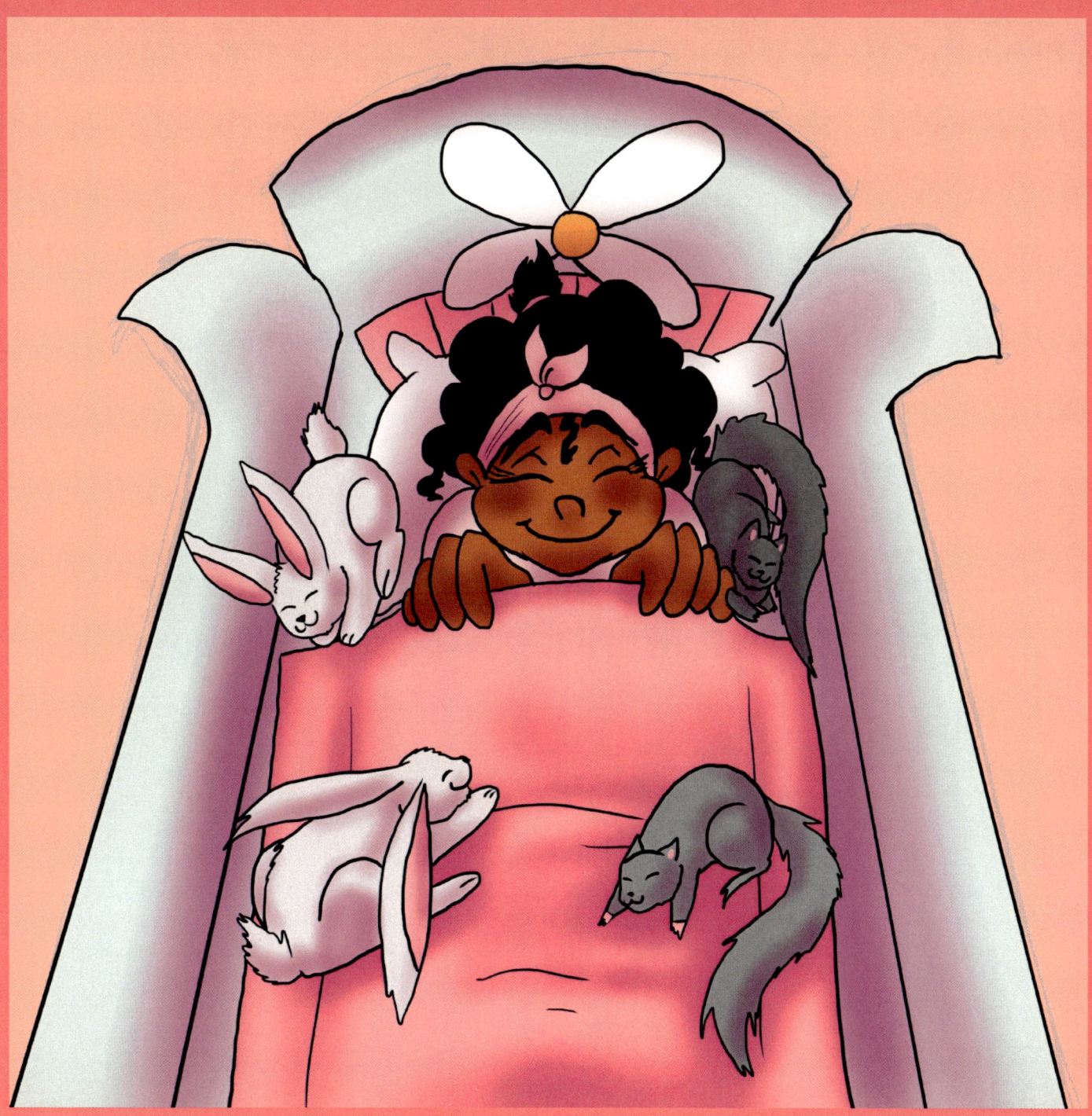

Mommy wakes her with a nudge and a smile. She says, "Kori, Mommy has a big surprise for you tonight." Kori leaps into mommy's arms excited and heads to the kitchen for breakfast.

All day long Kori thought about what her surprise would be. A new blanket? Maybe a new stuffed animal to add to her magical crib? Kori couldn't imagine the surprise that was waiting for her.

Bedtime came and mommy carried Kori to her room. As she opened the door, Kori noticed her magical crib was gone. In its place was a big girl bed. Kori becomes sad and thinks her adventures have come to an end.

All of a sudden she hears a vroom vroom! Kori becomes afraid as she looks over the side of the bed. She notices her big girl bed has a set of wheels. Kori smiles and sits back in the middle of the bed. She picks up her pillow as it turns into a steering wheel.

The bed jolts forward and travels up the wall. It glides easily around the dresser, coming to a screeching halt back in its resting place. Kori puts her pillow behind her head and lays back thinking, *this might not be so bad after all*

About the Author

Meiha Maxwell is a hardworking mother and wife from around the way. She has a bachelor's in psychology. Writing poetry was an escape for her as a child. Meiha loves to tap into her imagination and wrote about the impossibly possible. Meiha is an accomplished daydreamer. Her stories all begin with an outrageous thought about something incredibly normal

Made in United States
Orlando, FL
29 February 2024

44226955R00015